Butterfly Meadow

Mallow's Top Team

Olivia Moss

Illustrated by Sam Chaffey

■SCHOLASTIC

With special thanks to Sue Mongredien

First published in the UK in 2008 by Scholastic Children's Books
An imprint of Scholastic Ltd
Euston House, 24 Eversholt Street
London, NW1 1DB, UK
Registered office: Westfield Road, Southam, Warwickshire, CV47 0RA
SCHOLASTIC and associated logos are trademarks
and/or registered trademarks of Scholastic Inc.
Series created by Working Partners Ltd.

Text copyright © Working Partners, 2008
Illustration copyright © Sam Chaffey, 2008

The moral right of the author and illustrator of this work
has been asserted by them.

Cover illustration © Sam Chaffey, 2008

ISBN 978 1 407 10656 4

A CIP catalogue record for this book
is available from the British Library

Printed by
CPI Bookmarque, Croydon, CR0 4TD
Papers used by Scholastic Children's Books are made
from wood grown in sustainable forests.

1 3 5 7 9 10 8 6 4 2

www.scholastic.co.uk/zone

To Hannah Powell

CONTENTS

CHAPTER 1   Talent Search   1

CHAPTER 2   Picking Teams   7

CHAPTER 3   Dance Practise   15

CHAPTER 4   The Big Parade   23

CHAPTER 5   Watch Out!   31

CHAPTER 6   Dazzle's Big Chance   37

CHAPTER 7   Fast and Small   45

CHAPTER 8   The Real Reward   53

CHAPTER ONE

Talent Search

"...Eight, nine, ten! Ready or not, here I come!" called Dazzle. She was playing hide-and-seek with her best friend, Skipper, in Butterfly Meadow. Dazzle looked around, hoping to spot a flash of Skipper's blue wings. There was no sign of her friend. Where was Skipper hiding?

Dazzle fluttered through the air, searching the tall feathery grasses and colourful flowers. Ah! There was a splash of blue in the tall grass. Was it Skipper?

She dipped low for a closer look. No, it was a clump of bright cornflowers! Their blue heads were turned to the sun as they swayed in the gentle breeze.

Dazzle flew towards a patch of violet flowers. Maybe Skipper was hiding there. "I'm coming to find you!" she sang out, hoping her friend would giggle in reply.

Instead, a different butterfly's voice called out behind her. "All right, Team Butterfly. Let's G-O. Go!"

Dazzle turned in surprise as a cloud of colourful butterflies swirled up from some nearby flowers, chattering and laughing. What was all the excitement about?

Skipper darted out from where she'd been hiding in the rambling rose. "Come on!" she cried.

"What's going on?" Dazzle asked, confused.

"Today is Sports Day," Skipper explained. "You know Mallow, the Cabbage White butterfly over there. She's organizing it, just like she organized the party on your first

2

day at Butterfly Meadow!"

Dazzle and Skipper joined the circle of butterflies hovering around Mallow. "Quiet, please!" Mallow called. *She may be a small butterfly but she's got a BIG voice*, Dazzle thought, laughing to herself. "Hi everyone!" Mallow cried. "Today is our big Sports Day! We'll have the chance to compete

against all the other creatures at Cowslip Pond."

"Will we have races, like last time?" asked Spot, a red-and-black butterfly.

"Of course," Mallow replied. "Speed races, obstacle races, backwards flying races, you name it. And we've added a butterfly dance contest, too."

Skipper's wings quivered with excitement. "Can anyone take part?" she asked.

"Absolutely!" cried Mallow. "Everyone has a special talent. All you have to do is decide which event you want to try. Then we can fly to Cowslip Pond and start practising!"

Dazzle could hardly keep still. The air filled with eager voices as all the butterflies began chattering.

"Wow! I can't wait!" a tiny green butterfly shouted, bouncing on the breeze.

"I wonder who'll win the racing this time," another butterfly said.

A white butterfly with black spots on her wings turned to Dazzle. "Which race are *you* going to enter?" she asked. "Long-distance? Short sprint? Or maybe one of the obstacle races?"

Dazzle stopped short. "Um..." she replied. "I don't know."

"You don't know?" the spotted butterfly echoed.

Dazzle wasn't sure what to say. If everyone had a special talent, then she must have one, too. But she had no idea what it was!

CHAPTER TWO

Picking Teams

Dazzle glanced at Skipper, who was zipping back and forth between two tall plants. "What are you going to do at Sports Day?" Dazzle asked her friend.

"Race!" Skipper replied. "Maybe a short one, like the ten-lily-pad dash. How about you?"

Dazzle hesitated. Everyone else seemed so sure about what they wanted to do. "I don't know," she said.

Skipper touched the tip of her wing to Dazzle's. "Don't worry," she said kindly.

"I'm sure you'll find something. It's like Mallow said – everyone has a special talent."

Skipper was right. There must be something she was good at! Then she remembered her first party at Butterfly Meadow, where she'd learned to dance. She felt a sudden rush of happiness. "Maybe I'll try out for the dance contest," she replied.

Twinkle, a beautiful Peacock butterfly, whizzed by. A black-and-red patterned butterfly was flying right behind her. When she saw Skipper and Dazzle, Twinkle skidded to a stop. The other butterfly had to swerve sharply to avoid bumping into her. "Hey!" he yelled.

Twinkle turned around. "Oh, sorry," she said, waving a wing. "Hi there!" she cried to Dazzle and Skipper. "Have you met Stripe? He's a Red Admiral, and is very fast. Stripe, these are my best friends – Dazzle and Skipper."

Stripe gave a little bow, bobbing in the air. "Hi," he said. "Nice to meet you."

"Hello," Dazzle replied, looking at his wings in admiration. Stripe had red bands around the bottom and top of his wings, with white markings at the tips.

"Anyone want to race?" Stripe asked, zipping up into the air. "Come on, race me to the ash tree! Ready, set, go!"

Before Dazzle knew it, Stripe had flown off in a blur of red. Skipper zoomed quickly after him. Dazzle fluttered her wings too, trying to catch up. She flapped her wings as hard as she could, but before she'd got very far, she saw that Stripe had already looped around the ash tree and was flying back.

"Whew!" Dazzle laughed as he returned, with Skipper close behind. "You *are* fast. I guess you'll be racing on Sports Day too, right?"

"You bet!" Stripe said with a grin.

Just then, Mallow appeared. "The very butterflies I was looking for!" she declared. "I've signed up for the relay race.

Now all I need are three other butterflies for my team." She glanced around. "Stripe, Twinkle, Skipper – you're all fast fliers. Will you be on my team?"

"Sure," Twinkle agreed at once. "I'm in!" Then she paused. "What is a relay race, anyway?"

"Each member of the team flies a part of the distance," Mallow explained. "When one racer reaches the next racer, he or she passes a petal. Once the petal has been given to the last butterfly, she heads to the finish line. First over the line wins!"

"I've never tried the relay before," Stripe said. "It sounds like fun."

"And I'd love to be in the team, too," Skipper said.

Dazzle felt her antennae droop. She'd already decided to enter the dance contest, but she couldn't help feeling left out as the four butterflies huddled for a talk.

Skipper turned and gave Dazzle an encouraging smile. "You're going to enter the dance contest, aren't you, Dazzle?" she said.

"Yes, that's right." Dazzle grinned and showed Skipper her best twirl.

"Cool," Mallow said. Then she flew up high into the air. "Come on, butterflies!" she called. "Let's go to Cowslip Pond!"

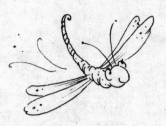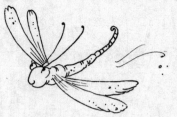

CHAPTER THREE

Dance Practice

Mallow led all the butterflies across the meadow and through the valley.

Cowslip Pond was already buzzing when they arrived. Water skaters twirled across the surface of the pond, practising a complicated routine on their spindly legs. Dragonflies swerved back and forth through the reeds, their green-and-blue bodies shimmering. And striped bumblebees raced between the white, purple, and yellow irises, competing to collect the most pollen. "Keep going!" the bees' coach called from

the sidelines. "Good job!"

"This is amazing!" Dazzle exclaimed, gazing around. She heard a chirping sound on the other side of the pond.

"That must be the Cowslip Pond Cricket Band," Skipper said, pointing a wing.

Dazzle could see a bunch of pale brown insects. They each had long legs and two pairs of wings. She remembered meeting crickets on her last trip to Cowslip Pond! They were all rubbing their front wings together at the same time to make the chirping sound.

"They're making music for the dancers," Mallow added. "The dancers are all meeting over on that side of the pond, Dazzle."

Dazzle wriggled her wings. "I'd better go join them," she said. "See you later."

"Bye, Dazzle," Skipper said, waving an antenna.

"OK, team, it's time to practise," Mallow said, turning to the others. "We need to be the best at passing the petal. A good petal-pass is the secret to winning, you know. . ."

Her voice faded as Dazzle fluttered across the pond. There, the dancing butterflies had organized themselves into lines in the air. A huge amber-coloured Monarch butterfly was giving instructions.

"And flap and turn and dive to your right!" called the Monarch. She spotted Dazzle. "Are you here to dance? Great! I'm Tawny. Join in whenever you're ready!"

Dazzle joined a line and tried to follow Tawny's instructions. She had never done a routine like this before!

"Now loop-the-loop . . . one, two, three, up!" Tawny chanted.

The air was full of colour. More butterflies than Dazzle could count all spun at once. She had never seen anything like it! She slowed down to watch a small turquoise butterfly do a perfect pirouette. But then Dazzle forgot to watch where she was going and. . .

Oh no! Dazzle bumped into an orangey-red butterfly with pale blue spots along the edges of its wings. Their wings tangled together, and both butterflies swung through the air.

"That's an interesting new move!" Tawny laughed at the front of the group.

"Oops!" Dazzle giggled as the orangey-red butterfly untangled itself. "Sorry."

"Not a problem," the butterfly replied, smiling.

"Now, left for three ... and right for three. . ." called Tawny. "Keep up in the back!"

Was Tawny talking to her? Dazzle tried hard to keep up as the other butterflies all rose and fell together.

She flew up . . . just as the others all flew down! "My name's Honey," the orangey-red butterfly whispered to Dazzle. "Don't worry, you'll get the hang of it soon." "I'm Dazzle," Dazzle replied, bumping into the brown butterfly in front of her. "Oops!" Trying to talk and dance at the same time was impossible. Dazzle concentrated on following Tawny's directions, but the harder she tried, the more mixed up she got.

20

"This way!" Honey called out helpfully as Tawny instructed the group to flutter in a circle. "Just follow me, Dazzle."

Dazzle was grateful that Honey was there to help her. Flying in a circle sounded easy, but it was actually pretty tricky.

"OK, let's take a break," Tawny said. The crickets fell silent. All the butterflies fluttered down to rest on the flowers at the side of the pond.

Dazzle and Honey were sipping nectar when Tawny flew up to them. "Dazzle, you'll make a wonderful backup flier for the dance contest," she said. "Thanks for all your hard work. I'll let you know if we need you for the competition."

21

"Oh," said Dazzle quietly. "Does that mean I didn't make the team?"

Tawny shook her head. "Not this time, dear. Sorry," she said.

CHAPTER FOUR

The Big Parade

Dazzle said goodbye to Honey and flew away, feeling disappointed. She decided to see what Skipper and the others were doing. Maybe it would cheer her up!

She found Skipper hovering in mid-air near the edge of the pond. "I'm waiting for Twinkle," Skipper explained. "We're practising our relay race. Oh. Here she comes! I'd better get ready."

Twinkle was coming up fast behind Skipper, carrying a long white daisy petal. "Here!" she cried, passing the petal to Skipper.

Skipper took it, then
streaked away like a bright blue line
along the edge of the pond. "Go, Skipper!"
Twinkle called after her. Then she turned to
Dazzle. "Didn't my wings look magnificent
as I flew? I must have been quite a sight."

Dazzle hid a smile. Twinkle was very proud of her large red wings. They had beautiful blue, purple, and pale yellow circles on them. "Oh yes," Dazzle told her friend. "You were, Twinkle."

The two butterflies watched as Skipper passed the petal to Stripe.

He flew the third stretch of the pond and thrust the petal at Mallow. She fumbled to get a hold of it,

then set off for the last leg of the race.

"We're still not fast enough," Twinkle said, sighing. "Not as fast as them, anyway." She pointed a wing.

Dazzle looked to see another team of butterflies whizzing around the pond. "Who are they?" she asked.

"Those are our rivals," Twinkle replied. "Spark, Buzz, Sizzle and Zing. They're *speedy*."

Spark, Buzz, Sizzle and Zing? Even their names sound fast! thought Dazzle. She watched as the butterflies zoomed through the air. Their heads were down, their wings were flapping so fast you could barely see them, and they were passing a golden buttercup petal.

Twinkle returned to her position for another practice race, and Dazzle wondered what to do next. It seemed like everyone had something to do at Sports Day – except her.

"Good afternoon, Cowslip Pond!" a large brown toad croaked. "Sports Day is about to begin. All spectators, please take their seats to watch the opening ceremony!"

Dazzle was feeling a little better now. She had made friends with Buddy, a lacewing beetle. He wouldn't be taking part in Sports Day either, because he had a torn wing. They sat together on a mossy log near the pond to watch.

The parade started with the frogs. They hopped around the wet grass, croaking with excitement. The newts waddled behind them, their tails swishing. Then the insects sitting near Dazzle and Buddy waved their feelers and cheered. The bugs were up next! Their hard shells shone in the sun. Up above flew hundreds of butterflies, a rainbow of colours against the blue sky. Dazzle spotted her friends in the group and waved her antennae at them.

 27

"Skipper! Twinkle!" she called. "Over here!" Skipper and Twinkle grinned and fluttered their wings in her direction.

"Here come the dragonflies," said Buddy. "Aren't they awesome?"

Dazzle gazed at the beautiful dragonflies, skimming through the air at the end of the parade. Their wings shimmered with all the colours of the rainbow.

Finally, the queen bee flew gracefully through the air and came to a stop right above the centre of Cowslip Pond. She looked around, her nose tipped up slightly in the air. Her golden stripes glowed in the sunlight.

"Let the games begin!" she declared.

CHAPTER FIVE

Watch Out!

Dazzle and Buddy watched the first events eagerly. The frogs had a long-jump contest, then the grasshoppers competed in the high jump. A praying mantis was trying to find someone to wrestle, but nobody dared to go near its deadly jaws!

"It must be kidding," Buddy whispered to Dazzle. "Wrestle with the scariest creature of Cowslip Pond? No thanks!"

Next was the diving beetles' deep-dive contest in the pond. "Look," Buddy said, pointing a feeler towards the water. "See how the beetles tuck bubbles of air under their wings? That's how they can breathe underwater."

"Cool," Dazzle said, impressed with everything her new friend was teaching her.

Then it was time for the butterfly dance contest. Dazzle and Buddy fell silent as they watched the group of beautiful butterflies all dancing in perfect unison. Dazzle was happy to see that her friend Honey didn't make a single mistake. "I tried out for the dance routine," Dazzle told Buddy, "but I wasn't good enough."

"Don't worry," Buddy said. "I'm sure you're good at lots of other things."

Just then, Dazzle noticed how high the sun was in the sky. It was almost time for

her friends' relay race! She decided to go and check up on them. "I'll be back soon," she told Buddy, fluttering off to the practice area.

As Dazzle flew up, she could hear Mallow shouting a special cheer:

> *"Mallow, Twinkle, Skipper, and Stripe;*
> *We're the best racers, the fastest ones!"*

Dazzle landed on a plant nearby. "That doesn't rhyme," Twinkle said to Mallow and Dazzle. "Aren't cheers supposed to rhyme?"

"How about, 'the fastest type' instead of 'the fastest ones'?" Dazzle suggested. "That would make it rhyme."

"Good job, Dazzle!" Mallow said, nodding her head.

> *"Mallow, Skipper, Stripe, and Twinkle;*
> *We're the best racers, the fastest type!"*

"You got the names in the wrong order!"

Skipper giggled. "It still doesn't rhyme."

"OK, OK." Stripe said, sighing. "We need to practise. The relay is the big finale of Sports Day, and everyone will be watching. We've got to win!"

"He's right," Twinkle agreed. "Take your positions, butterflies!"

The four butterflies fluttered to their starting places. Twinkle flew first, passing the petal to Skipper. Skipper zoomed around to Stripe. Stripe took the petal and raced to Mallow. Finally, Mallow grabbed the petal and set off along the last part of the loop.

"Faster, Mallow, faster!" Stripe cheered.

Dazzle could see Mallow flap her wings even harder, trying to speed up. But as she rounded the final turn, a dragonfly appeared from out of nowhere.

CRASH!

Mallow flew right into the dragonfly – then tumbled to the ground! She didn't move. Was Mallow hurt?

CHAPTER SIX

Dazzle's Big Chance

Dazzle rushed over to her friend. "Mallow!" she cried. "Are you OK?"

Mallow seemed dazed. "My head is spinning," she said feebly.

Stripe flew over and checked Mallow's wings for rips or tears. "Nothing's broken," he said. "Can you fly?"

Mallow got up slowly, her wings trembling. She tried to fly but tumbled back to the ground again. "Sorry," she said quietly. "I feel a little shaky. I need to take a rest."

Skipper and Twinkle had arrived by now. "What's going on?" Skipper asked.

"I don't think I'll be able to fly in the race," Mallow told them sadly.

"Oh, no!" Twinkle cried.

"Do we have to drop out?" Stripe asked.

"Well, it's too late to find a new team member," Skipper said. "Unless. . ." She turned to Dazzle. "Unless *you* could take Mallow's place?"

Dazzle stared, surprised. "Me? But I'm not fast enough," she replied.

Twinkle, who was helping Mallow up, interrupted. "Oh, please say you'll do it!" she begged.

Stripe bent a flower over, so that Mallow could reach it and drink some nectar. "The team needs four racers," he said. "The race starts soon, and we don't have time to find anyone else."

"I don't know," Dazzle said uncertainly. "You've practised so hard! I don't want to let you all down."

"You won't," Twinkle told her. "I saw how fast you flew here when Mallow got hurt. You're faster than you think."

"And I can coach you," Mallow said, between sips of nectar. "Please?"

Dazzle hesitated, then nodded. "I'll try my best," she said.

Skipper, Twinkle, Stripe and Mallow all cheered. "That's the spirit!" said Twinkle.

Stripe looked at Dazzle seriously. "There's no time to lose."

"You'll be flying the last part of the race," Skipper said.

"And I'll be passing the petal to you," Stripe added, picking up the daisy petal. "Let's give it a try."

Dazzle and Stripe practised. At first, Dazzle had trouble taking the petal and flying at the same time.

"Don't worry," Mallow said. "Once you get the hang of it, you'll be able to do it without thinking."

Mallow was right! It only took Dazzle a few more tries to learn what to do. Stripe flew up close to Dazzle's side. Then Dazzle started flying the minute she had the petal. She and Stripe tried the petal-pass again and again, faster and faster.

"That's good," said Mallow. "Remember to keep your antennae and body in a straight line, like an arrow, when you fly. And flap your wings in fast, small strokes."

"Got it," Dazzle said, practising. *Fast and small, fast and small*, she murmured to herself as she sped along. The wind rushed past her. She never realized how great it felt to fly fast! The speed made her feel all giggly.

"Oh, and Dazzle?" called Mallow. "The most important thing to remember is to have fun. That's what today is all about."

"I'll try," Dazzle said nervously. It was strange how she felt scared and excited all at the same time.

Just then, an announcement boomed out across the pond. "Would all butterflies competing in the team relay race make their way to their starting positions, please?"

"We're on!" Stripe cried. "Let's go, guys. Time to show Spark and his team a thing or two."

"Good luck, Dazzle," Mallow called, flying carefully towards a spot where she could sit and watch the race. "I'll cross my antennae for you."

"Thanks," Dazzle said, taking a deep breath. "I'll do my best." *I won't let my friends down*, she vowed to herself as she flew. They had all been so nice, welcoming her to Butterfly Meadow and helping her fit in. Now it was her turn to be a good friend to them!

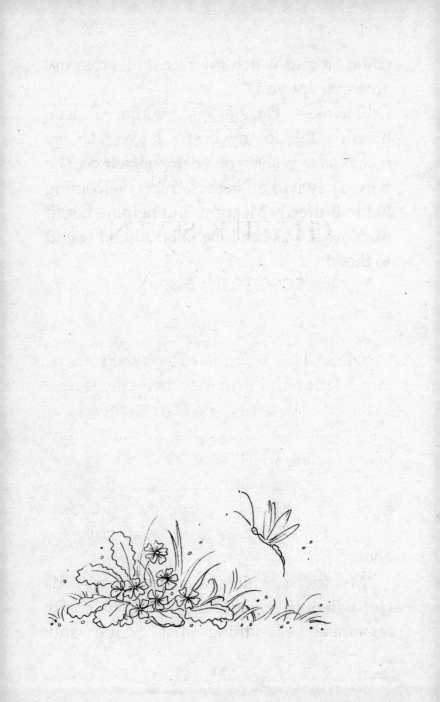

CHAPTER SEVEN

Fast and Small

Dazzle and her teammates took their places around the pond with the other relay teams. Three other butterflies lined up in the fourth relay position alongside Dazzle. Buzz, from Spark's team, was there.

Buzz cocked an antenna at Dazzle. "I've never seen you race before," he said. "But if you're in Stripe's team, you must be good."

"My friends think so," Dazzle replied. Her wings trembled. She hoped she could remember everything that Stripe and

Mallow had taught her. If she was slow, they wouldn't win and she'd let her friends down. That would be awful!

One of the frogs let out a loud croak to signal the start of the race. And they were off! Four butterflies bolted into action and soared around the pond. Twinkle was one of them, flying as fast as her pretty wings would take her. Twinkle reached Skipper and passed her the petal. Skipper zoomed away, but made the mistake of looking behind her, which slowed her down. "Keep going, Skipper!" Dazzle called.

All of the spectators cheered for their favourite teams. "Fly, Zing, fly!" Dazzle heard some ladybirds yelling.

Skipper caught up with Zing, from Spark's team, and stayed next to him for their leg of the race. Then she passed the petal to Stripe, who bolted ahead. He flew clear of the whole pack!

The audience was getting really excited now. The frogs hopped up and down, croaking loudly. The newts stomped their feet. And the insects chirped, cheered and shouted!

"Go, Stripe! Go, Stripe!" a group of black-and-white butterflies chanted from the stands.

Stripe was getting closer to Dazzle, flying faster than she'd ever seen him fly before. Dazzle moved into position to grab the petal. Stripe seemed to be having trouble slowing down. *Maybe that's normal*, Dazzle thought. But he was heading straight for her!

"Whoa!" Stripe yelled . . . as he bumped right into Dazzle!

No one was hurt, but Stripe tumbled up ahead. Dazzle had to zoom to catch up with him and grab the petal. Meanwhile, Buzz had flown into the lead. Oh, no! Dazzle's team was losing. It was all up to her now. She *had* to get back in the race.

Fast and small, fast and small, Dazzle

reminded herself, as she flapped her wings. But Buzz was still up in front of her, his purple wings beating even faster.

Then, through the cheers of the crowd, Dazzle heard a familiar voice:

*"Dazzle, Twinkle, Skipper, and Stripe
You're the best racers, the fastest type!"*

It was Mallow. She had changed her cheer to include Dazzle's name!

Dazzle found an extra burst of energy. She flew even faster, and pulled level with Buzz. She could see the finish line up ahead.

Come on, Dazzle!
she told herself. Her wings
were starting to feel tired, but with one
final push, she bolted ahead of Buzz at the
last second. Her team had won the race!

CHAPTER EIGHT

The Real Reward

Dazzle felt dizzy with excitement. She could hardly believe it. Stripe, Twinkle, Mallow and Skipper flew over to celebrate, tapping their wings together joyfully. The crowd cheered. Dazzle could see Buddy in the audience, clapping his antennae and beaming proudly.

"I knew you could do it," Skipper told Dazzle, grinning.

"Great job, Dazzle," Mallow said. "Seeing you race across that finish line made me feel a whole lot better."

"It was your cheer that helped me go faster," Dazzle told Mallow. "That was just what I needed!"

The queen bee hovered above the centre of the pond again, and the crowd fell silent. "What a wonderful Sports Day," she said. "Everyone who's participated is a winner, but special congratulations go to those who came first in their events."

The audience applauded as the queen bee circled the pond, handing out awards. As she approached Dazzle and her team,

Dazzle was so excited she could hardly keep her wings still!

Dazzle glanced around and spotted Mallow watching from a nearby plant. "Mallow, come here," she called to the little white butterfly. "You're the one who put this team together in the first place. We wouldn't have won without you!"

Mallow flew over to join the team as the queen bee came to a stop in front of them. Mallow smiled at Dazzle. "Thank you, Dazzle," she whispered. "You did a lot to help our team today."

The queen bee gave Dazzle, Skipper, Twinkle, Stripe and Mallow a touch of golden pollen on their wings. "You all did very well," she told them. "What an exciting race!"

Dazzle felt as if she might burst with pride. "Thank you," she managed to say,

dipping her head respectfully.

"Oh, look how the pollen sparkles on my wings!" Twinkle cried as they all flew back to the sidelines. "They're even more beautiful than usual."

Dazzle smiled. She loved how the golden pollen shimmered on her yellow wings too,

but for her, the real reward had been racing with her friends and being part of a team. She would never forget that!

"Three cheers for Sports Day," Mallow called out. "Hip hip. . ."

"HOORAY!" cried all the creatures around Cowslip Pond.

"Hip hip. . ."

"HOORAY!"

"Hip hip. . ."

"HOORAY!"

Dazzle twirled in the air, bursting with happiness. It had been a perfect day with her friends – one that she would never forget.

Want to know all about the butterflies
in the meadow?

Dazzle

Pale Clouded Yellow butterfly

Likes: Dancing and making friends

Dislikes: Being left out

Twinkle

Peacock butterfly

Likes: Her beautiful wings

Dislikes: Getting wet!

Mallow

Cabbage White butterfly

Likes: Organizing parties and activities

Dislikes: Being bored

Skipper

Holly Blue butterfly

Likes: Helping others

Dislikes: Birds who try to eat her!

Read about more adventures in
Butterfly Meadow

FLUTTERY, FRIENDLY FUN

Butterfly Meadow

Dazzle's First Day

Olivia Moss

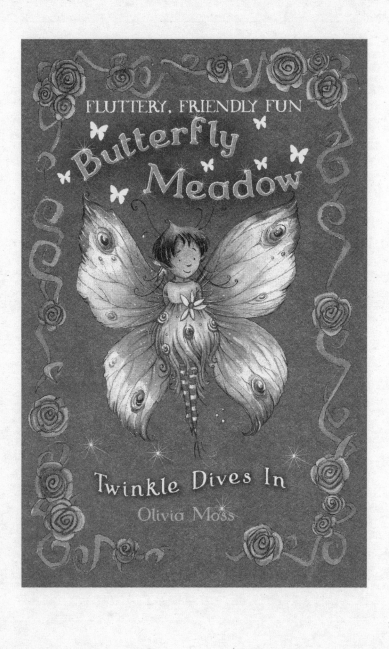

FLUTTERY, FRIENDLY FUN

Butterfly Meadow

Twinkle Dives In

Olivia Moss

FLUTTERY, FRIENDLY FUN

Butterfly Meadow

Skipper to the Rescue

Olivia Moss

And coming soon

FLUTTERY, FRIENDLY FUN

Butterfly Meadow

Dazzle's Prickly Problem

Olivia Moss

FLUTTERY, FRIENDLY FUN

Butterfly Meadow

Twinkle and the Busy Bee

Olivia Moss